Isla OF ADVENTURE

THE SECRET CABANA

by Dela Costa   **illustrated by Ana Sebastián**

LITTLE SIMON

New York London Toronto Sydney New Delhi

LITTLE SIMON

An imprint of Simon & Schuster Children's Publishing Division

1230 Avenue of the Americas, New York, New York 10020

First Little Simon paperback edition December 2022

Copyright © 2022 by Simon & Schuster, Inc.

All rights reserved, including the right of reproduction in whole or in part in any form.

LITTLE SIMON is a registered trademark of Simon & Schuster, Inc., and associated colophon is a trademark of Simon & Schuster, Inc. For information about special discounts for bulk purchases, please contact Simon & Schuster Special Sales at 1-866-506-1949 or business@simonandschuster.com.

The Simon & Schuster Speakers Bureau can bring authors to your live event. For more information or to book an event contact the Simon & Schuster Speakers Bureau at 1-866-248-3049 or visit our website at www.simonspeakers.com.

Series designed by Laura Roode.

Book designed by Laura Roode. The text of this book was set in Congenial.

Manufactured in the United States of America 1122 LAK

10 9 8 7 6 5 4 3 2 1

Cataloging-in-Publication Data is available for this title from the Library of Congress.

ISBN 978-1-6659-2657-7 (hc)

ISBN 978-1-6659-2656-0 (pbk)

ISBN 978-1-6659-2658-4 (ebook)

Contents

ABUELO'S HERE!

◆◇◆◇◆◇◆◇◆◇◆◇◆

"Hey, Isla," said Fitz. "If a piece of blueberry pancake accidentally falls off your plate, I'd be happy to take care of it for you."

Isla Verde laughed at her little gecko buddy. They had been best friends for as long as Isla had known she could speak to animals. Which was a very long time—basically all eight years of her life.

1

"You have your own papaya slices," Isla said.

"True. But there's always room for more," Fitz said.

Then Isla heard a cheerful whistle that she knew very well. It was her abuelo!

"He's early!" Fitz said in a panic. "I thought I had time for a nap or two before we left."

"No time for napping," Isla replied. "The cabana is waiting!"

"*Cielo*, are you ready?" Mama asked between sips of freshly brewed coffee.

Coffee was one of the adult mysteries Isla couldn't solve. It tasted gross, but grown-ups loved it. Maybe she would change her mind when she was older.

"Ready as ever," Isla said as she got up and checked her vest pockets. She had her notebook, a pencil, and a few color markers. She was always ready for a little creative moment.

And in Sol, just about everything was inspiring.

"It smells delicious in here," said a familiar kind voice. "I should have come earlier!"

"ABUELO!" said Isla as she ran to her grandpa and hugged him tightly.

"Good morning, *chicas*!" said Abuelo. "And Fitz, of course."

Fitz sat on Isla's empty plate with a hand on his very full belly. "I need a minute. So full . . . of pancakes."

Abuelo wasn't like other grandpas. He was a nature scientist, and today he was dressed for fieldwork. He wore rolled-up pants, a vest with lots of pockets, a bucket hat, and old boots. And he never left home without his compass and binoculars.

Isla pointed to her own outfit. "We're matching!"

Abuelo let out a deep laugh. *"Perfecto! Let's get going, then. I'll help your mama with snacks. Why don't you and Fitz wait by the car and think about what music we should play?"*

Isla scooped up Fitz, kissed Mama goodbye, and headed outside.

The bright sunshine was warm. A light breeze waved hello. And Isla's new neighbor, Tora Rosa, was on a mission of her own.

"Um, why is Tora on her porch with a magnifying glass?" Fitz asked. "I thought she only looked at mirrors."

"I don't know," said Isla. "But there's one way to find out."

TO THE CABANA

◊◊◊◊◊◊◊◊◊◊◊◊◊◊

Isla skipped up to the porch where her brightly-dressed friend sat.

"Whatcha doing?" Isla asked.

Tora sighed with relief. "Thank goodness you're here! I am so bored! I mean, this is my third outfit today, my second hairstyle, and now I'm watching ants carry crumbs."

Fitz shivered. "How . . . fun."

Tora smiled at the gecko's reaction. "See, I don't speak to animals, but even I know Fitz *feels* my boredom."

Isla laughed. "Well, we're heading to the family beach cabana. You should come."

Tora dropped the magnifying glass and shrieked. "Yes! Please! Let's go right now!"

Isla peeked at her friend's squeaky-clean sandals. "Maybe you should change first. You wouldn't want the sand to ruin your shoes."

"These old things?" Tora wiggled a foot. "They're *so* last season!"

Fitz snickered. "The girl knows her fashion."

"Let me go ask my mom," Tora said, already halfway to the front door.

"And I'll let Abuelo know we'll have one more on the trip," Isla said.

"I told you there was always room for more," Fitz said proudly.

"But you were talking about pancakes," said Isla.

"Pancakes, best friends . . . what's the difference?" said Fitz. "I love them both!"

When everyone was ready, the three friends piled into Abuelo's car and put on their seatbelts.

Tora brought a heart-shaped backpack with her, and she also brought a bright smile.

"It's nice to meet you, Mr. Verde!" she said. "I'm Tora."

"It's wonderful to meet you, too, Señorita Tora," said Abuelo. "What's in that beautiful bag of yours?"

He clearly said the right thing. Tora's eyes sparkled as she listed items with her hands. "Thanks for noticing! I brought sunglasses . . . sunscreen . . . hand sanitizer . . . bug spray . . . backup hand sanitizer . . . and a camera."

"A camera!" Isla clapped her hands.
"We'll take tons of pictures!"

"Sounds like we're ready for
adventure," Abuelo said.

And the best friends in the back seat
agreed!

CHAPTER 3

THE LEGEND
OF CANTO COAST

◆◆◆◆◆◆◆◆◆◆◆◆◆◆

The car ride was filled with long island roads and music.

The girls sang along loudly. Isla was okay at singing, but Tora surprised everyone with her voice.

"Wow, you sound like a real pop star!" Isla cheered.

Tora smiled bashfully. "Aw, thanks. I used to take lessons."

"I've only taken swimming lessons," Isla said. "My teacher was a dolphin. Remember how fun that was, Fitz?"

"It was great! I slept on the sand the whole time," Fitz reminded her.

Tora pulled out her camera and took a
few pictures of trees and plants pouring
over onto the roads outside.

"Wow, it's so beautiful here," she
said.

Then they passed a sign. It read: CANTO COAST TO THE RIGHT. WATERFALLS TO THE LEFT.

"Waterfalls?" asked Tora. "You have waterfalls here?"

"We sure do," Abuelo replied with excitement. "But we are going to Canto Coast today. Now, do either of you know *why* it's called Canto Coast?"

Both girls shook their heads.

Abuelo continued, "Legend has it that a long, long time ago, even before I was born . . ."

"That *is* a long time," Fitz whispered.

"A sailor and a mermaid met there and fell in love," Abuelo finished.

"A mermaid?" Tora gasped. "First waterfalls, now *mermaids*? Isla, why didn't you tell me about this?"

Isla was surprised too. "Because I've never heard of it."

Abuelo turned down the music and said, "You don't know this legend? Then close your eyes and come with me, back to once upon a time, when mermaids lived in the waters of Sol.

"A young sailor was lost at sea during a storm. He was adrift in a lifeboat, and though he had a compass, he had no paddles to steer himself. So he waited for his crew to find him.

"Days passed and no one came. Then, just as the sailor was about to lose hope, a beautiful mermaid rose from the waves. She opened her mouth and a song spilled out. The song was so moving that the sailor's boat began floating toward a distant shore.

"On that coast, the sailor found food
and a secret cabana where he could live.
He also found the love of his life . . . the
mermaid.

"But mermaids cannot live on dry land, so when the sailor wished to see her, he sang the mermaid's song and she swam to the surface. *That* is why it's called Canto Coast."

Tora was breathless. "Because *canto* means song! We're going to the coast of the mermaid's song."

"But Abuelo," Isla said curiously, "that's just a made-up story."

Her grandpa shrugged. "Why can't it be real? Nature is a mystery, after all."

Isla knew all about that. But mermaids? Mermaids weren't real. Surely it was just a silly legend.

CHAPTER 4

PICTURE PERFECT

◆◆◆◆◆◆◆◆◆◆◆◆◆◆◆

The Verde family cabana was Isla's home away from home. Isla liked to think of it as a beach gazebo, with a triangular roof and large open windows. Seashells and sprouting beach grass decorated the front entrance.

"This is *so* much better than staring at ants all day," Tora said. "My parents *need* to get one of these."

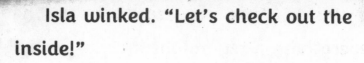

Isla winked. "Let's check out the inside!"

Abuelo followed the girls and gecko with a snack-filled cooler.

Inside, the breezy cabana had everything they might need for their visit. There were beanbags, a desk where Abuelo could work, a few buckets and pails, and pictures hanging on the walls.

Isla and Tora plopped down on the beanbags.

"What will you be working on today, Mr. Verde?" Tora asked.

"I'll collect water samples to make sure the water is clean," Abuelo explained. "It's important that we do our part and take care of our home."

Isla asked, "How can we help?"

"Why don't you girls have some fun?" Abuelo suggested. He reached into the cooler and handed out bags of sliced fruit. "Run around and explore."

Fitz stared at his snack bag hungrily. "You don't have to tell me twice!"

Abuelo went outside with a set of plastic tubes and a bucket to start his work.

Tora took out her camera. "Picture time! Say cheese, Fitz."

She turned to the gecko and snapped a photo of him stuffing his mouth. The camera made a whirring sound as the picture slowly printed out.

"Oh, this is gold!" Isla laughed. "Fitz, look at your face!"

Fitz swallowed his food. "I've never looked better. But is my tongue *really* that long?"

They took turns taking silly pictures of one another. Fitz snapped one of the girls doing cartwheels. Then

they used Tora's sunscreen to draw on each other's faces. Isla's favorite photo was of Tora and Fitz posing as if they were fashion models.

Isla knew this would be one of her favorite cabana memories.

"Let's go enjoy the sun," Fitz suggested. "I think I'm ready to lie down on the sand for a few gecko minutes."

Isla picked him up. "Tora, Fitz here thinks it's time for some classic fun in the sun. Why not bring the camera?"

Outside, Tora stared at the ocean with hopeful eyes. "I know you don't believe in mermaids, but I can't stop thinking about Abuelo's story. What if she showed up right now?"

Isla shrugged. "In a fairytale, I guess anything is possible."

Tora lifted her camera to her eyes to take a picture of the sea.

Then she gasped and dropped her camera. It landed safely on the sand, but Tora's eyes and mouth were wide open.

Isla bent down to pick up the camera. "Tora? Are you okay?"

"Over there!" Tora shouted, pointing at something in the water. "It's the mermaid of Canto Coast! She's real! She's real! I just *knew* she was real!"

Isla heard a loud splash in the water as she caught a glimmer of something in the sea. Something that looked like a large fin.

IS SEEING BELIEVING?

◆◇◆◇◆◇◆◇◆◇◆◇◆◇◆

Tora was so thrilled by what she saw that she was ready to leap in the water and swim after it.

"That had to be the mermaid!" Tora yelled with excitement. "You saw it too, Isla! You saw her shiny tail!"

"I saw something," said Isla, who didn't want to disappoint her friend. "But it could have been a dolphin."

"Or a really, really, really big fish," Fitz added.

Tora crossed her arms. "Even Abuelo thinks she might be real. Why are you so against mermaids existing?"

"I'm not *against* mermaids, I just think they're maybe more of a story," Isla said. "It's like saying Bigfoot is real."

Tora threw her hands in the air. "No one has been able to prove Bigfoot *isn't* real!"

Fitz gulped. "If he is real, this gecko is getting outta here!"

"I wish you'd try to be a little more open-minded about this," Tora said with a bummed-out look. "I believed *your* secret about speaking to animals."

Fitz whispered, "She's got you there."

Isla looked down. She noticed that Fitz had been keeping score in the sand.

ISLA / TORA
0 / 2

Hmm, maybe I am being close-minded, Isla thought.

Then she turned to her friend and said, "You're right, Tora. On Sol, the best discoveries are made when you search for the impossible. So let's find some clues and solve this mermaid mystery."

"Really?" gasped Tora. "Fabulous! Okay, where should we start?"

"We could learn more about the legend," Fitz suggested.

Isla faced Tora with determination in her eyes. "Okay! Fitz says we should get more info. But we're going to need to ask questions and gather data. We need names, places—anything that will help."

Tora squealed and hugged Isla. "Abuelo might know more. Let's go ask him."

"Actually," Isla said, "I was thinking we should ask some of the locals. You know, the ones who live here on the beach."

It took Tora a moment to catch Isla's meaning. "Oh! You mean, the *animal* locals."

Isla winked. "Exactly! Now, who would normally be hanging around the beach all night and day?"

"I've got an answer, but you're not going to like it," said Fitz.

"No, don't say it," Isla begged.

"Yep," said Fitz. "I think you need to start with . . . the hermit crabs."

Isla let out a groan. *Anything but the hermit crabs*, she thought.

THE SECRET LIFE OF HERMIT CRABS

◆◆◆◆◆◆◆◆◆◆◆◆◆◆

Here was the deal with hermit crabs.

First, privacy was a big deal to the little critters.

Second, they were always moving things around! They never stood still for too long.

And finally, you could never expect to get any answers without giving something back in return.

Isla gave Tora a few pointers as they searched for crabs. "A group of hermit crabs is called a cluster. And it's usually best to ask easy questions. They can get a little . . ."

"Crabby?" Tora giggled.

"Pretty much," Isla said. "Oh, look!"

Just ahead, hermit crabs were crawling over a huge pile of glittering seashells. Isla liked to collect shells and bring them back to her bedroom. There were so many shapes and colors, not a single one was like the other! But it was always smart to make sure a crab wasn't living inside one first.

"Hi, friends!" Isla kneeled in the sand.

Tora also kneeled to say hello. "Wow, what beautiful shells!"

The hermit crabs immediately stopped their search for new homes. But instead of speaking back, they vanished inside their shells.

"Oh!" Tora squeaked. She looked around awkwardly. "Was it something I said?"

Isla sighed. "Don't worry. It takes a moment to get them out of their shells."

"I've got this." Fitz crawled down to the sand. Facing the hermit crabs, he put

his hands on his hips and puffed out his chest. "Now, listen here! We have some answers and you'd better question them!"

Isla raised an eyebrow. "Uh . . ."

Fitz shook his head. "Questions! We have questions that need answers!"

A tumbleweed of beach grass passed by. Not a single hermit crab popped out.

Tora opened her backpack and took out her fruit bag. "Maybe a snack will help."

"Well, why didn't you say you brought food with ya?" said a blue-shelled crab who peeked out and rushed over. "We're starving!"

Another one with a large, pointy shell joined them. "Is that coconut? I love coconut, but they are so hard to open."

"Hey, look! Food!" The other hermit crabs all emerged happily from their shells and skittered over to Tora.

She squeaked in surprise and spread out the fruit on the sand. "Ha! That was easy! One at a time, one at a time. There's plenty for everyone!"

"Great thinking, Tora," Isla whispered as she high-fived her friend.

"Now," the blue-shelled crab said, "what do ya need to know?"

CHAPTER 7

A MYSTERY SINGER

◊◊◊◊◊◊◊◊◊◊◊◊◊

Now that they had the attention of the hermit crabs, Isla didn't waste any time.

"I'm Isla and these are my friends, Fitz and Tora," she said. "What are your names?"

"I'm Blue," the blue-shelled crab said while eating. "That's Pointy."

Pointy waved a claw.

"That makes sense," Isla said.

She took out her notebook and a pencil to write down the names of her new friends. "Tora, Blue and Pointy here will be helping us out today."

"Nice to meet you." Tora smiled. "Hey, Isla, do you mind if I ask the questions? I've never really talked to hermit crabs before."

Isla beamed. "I think that's a great idea!"

Tora leaned down a little closer to the eating crabs. "Hello, Blue. Hello, Pointy. Have either of you ever heard a beautiful singing voice around here? It would be a voice so beautiful, you can't help but fall in love with it."

Blue nodded. "If you're looking for a singer, we've got one right here." He turned to the cluster behind them. "Hey, Joey, sing your crab song!"

A high-pitched voice from inside the group replied, "I retired! Ever since I almost got eaten by a bird, my voice hasn't been the same!"

"Well, that's terrifying!" Fitz said, glancing at the sky.

Isla told Tora what the crabs said, and they tried not to laugh.

"Sorry you had to retire, Joey," Tora said kindly. "I don't think we're looking for another crab, though. Any other ideas?"

"Hmm . . ." Pointy paused his chewing to think. "There *was* this one singer on the beach with a voice so beautiful, you'd give up your shell for it." Then he turned back to the cluster. "Hey, Joey!" he yelled. "Where was the singer you found last week?"

Joey shouted, "The secret cabana!"

"What he said," Pointy said.

This was all news to Isla. She had never heard of this mystery singer or this secret cabana. She quickly jotted down some notes. This mermaid search had become incredibly interesting!

"Could you point us in the right direction?" Isla asked.

Blue raised a claw and pointed to where the sand turned into dirt. Large palm trees loomed over the beach. "Go straight that way. Ya can't miss it."

"Tora," Isla said, "I think we may have found your mermaid's secret cabana."

"Thank you, thank you, thank you!" Tora gave the hermit crabs the rest of her fruit. "Blue, Pointy, would you mind if I took your picture? I never want to forget this!"

Blue retreated into his shell. "No, no! No pictures! I gotta get a new shell!"

Pointy tapped Blue with a claw. "Aw, come on. They're nice!"

"Fine," Blue grumbled after a moment. "Just make sure to get my good side."

Tora clicked her camera and the photo printed out. "You all look great!"

"Wow, a photo of a hermit crab out of their shell? You're lucky," Isla said. "Now, let's see if that luck lasts with finding this secret cabana!"

AN UNEXPECTED DISCOVERY

◇◇◇◇◇◇◇◇◇◇◇◇◇

Though they followed where the hermit crabs had pointed, they found absolutely nothing.

No singer. No beautiful mermaid. No secret cabana.

"I guess it's not the first wild goose chase a hermit crab has sent me on," Isla said.

"At least it's not as bad as the time

that real goose sent us on a wild goose chase," said Fitz.

"Oh yeah," said Isla. "Hmm, I'm beginning to think hermit crabs are not very good at giving directions."

"No! We can't give up," Tora announced. "Maybe the cabana is just hard to find. It *is* a secret, after all."

Fitz yawned. "All this searching for secret things is making me sleepy."

"Everything makes you sleepy," Isla reminded her gecko friend.

Then she closed her eyes and tried to picture Sol. Though Isla had explored almost every corner of her home, it was possible she'd missed a legendary detail.

A soft, enchanting melody interrupted her thoughts. Isla whipped her head toward the palm trees. Someone was there, singing.

Ah, ah, ahhhh . . . !

"Please tell me you hear that," Tora whispered. Her feet were already moving forward, as if the magical voice was pulling her closer.

Fitz was no longer sleepy. "It's the voice of an angel!"

"Not an angel . . . but maybe a mermaid," Isla said. She felt just as enchanted as her friends. A mermaid, here in Sol? Could it be true?

"Let's go!" Tora said, leading her friends into the palm tree grove.

As they walked, they pushed fallen palm tree fronds out of the way and did their best not to step on anyone or anything. Soon, they stumbled on a very old, hidden cabana.

Fitz rubbed his eyes. "I'll never doubt a hermit crab again!"

This cabana was similar to Isla's, but the roof was made of thatch and the door was a bit crooked.

"Should we go in?" Tora asked nervously.

Isla needed to think. "How does one greet a mermaid? I don't want to offend her."

"We should definitely bow. It's a sign of respect. See?" Tora bowed grandly, sweeping a hand to the side.

"Works for me!" Isla exclaimed.

Tora stepped forward and placed a hand on the door. It gave a whiny creak, startling the singer inside. The voice broke and missed a note in its beautiful song.

Isla paused. Maybe they were interrupting something. Maybe some secrets should *stay* hidden.

But Tora said, "It's now or never. My bow won't get any more perfect than this."

She pushed open the door with a great *whoosh*.

"Greetings, your great majesty of the sea. It is I, Tora Rosa of the humans. It is an honor to meet you," Tora said as she bowed deeply.

A familiar voice squawked back. "Finally! I am given the respect I deserve!"

YOU AGAIN!

◆◇◆◇◆◇◆◇◆◇◆◇◆

The three friends looked and saw something *even* more unexpected than a fairytale creature.

"Fabio?" Isla, Tora, and Fitz shrieked.

"Well, well, well! If it isn't Isla, Frankenstein, and their new friend, Tomato," Fabio said smugly.

"Was that *you* singing?" Tora asked in surprise.

Fabio put a wing to his chest, insulted. "Oh, Tomato, that was just *practice*. I've never sounded worse!"

"You're joking! You've never sounded *better*!" Fitz said.

Fabio ruffled his feathers in surprise. "Bah! Didn't you hear what I just said?"

"But why are you hidden away in here?" Isla asked. "There's no one to hear you sing."

All the cabana had to offer was stray

leaves, a few crawling bugs, and the music stand Fabio was perched on.

The seagull flew to a porthole window. "Why, the best teacher in the world is here!"

Isla waved Fitz and Tora over to stand beside Fabio.

"What are we supposed to be looking at?" Tora asked. "Besides the beach?"

"Not the beach, but my teacher—" Fabio stopped himself and flew back to the music stand. "You won't steal my secrets! Now, hear my voice! *LaaAAa! LAAaaAA!*"

The three friends covered their ears and groaned. Now *this* was the Fabio they knew.

All around them, the cabana shook with the horrible sound. Something fell from the thatched roof and crashed in the corner.

"What's this?" Tora asked as she picked up the object that fell and blew the dust away.

Fabio flew over and landed on top of Tora's head to get a better look. Then he leaned down and looked into her eyes. "Don't bother with that old clock. It has *never* worked."

"GAH!" screeched Tora as she waved
the bird away. "What's he doing?"

"He says it's a clock that doesn't
work," Isla explained.

"That's because it's not a clock," Tora said. "It's a compass, silly bird. It gives directions, not the time."

Fabio spread his wings wide open. "Why would I need some toy to give me directions? I'm the true compass of the sea! But I simply can't live without my broken clock, so be a good little Tomato and give it here."

Tora used her free hand to stop Fabio from taking the compass. "Isla, this could be the same compass the sailor used in the mermaid's tale!"

Isla looked at Fabio. "How about this? If you let us keep the compass, Tora will take pictures of you for your adoring fans."

"Imagine it, Fabio," Fitz said as he waved his gecko hands in the air. "Your face . . . all over town . . . for everyone to see."

That was all Fabio needed to hear before he started to pose dramatically. "Who am I to deny the town my beauty?"

Tora snapped a few photos of Fabio
and handed them over as they printed.
"Done deal!"

Fabio snatched the photos with his feet before flying away. "Have fun with your broken clock, Tomato! It only points one way!"

"What do you mean it only points one way?" Isla shouted as he disappeared into the sky.

Tora lifted the compass and moved it around. Fabio was right. It stayed true to one direction: toward the water.

CHAPTER 10

THE BEST DAY EVER

◇◇◇◇◇◇◇◇◇◇◇◇◇

Isla, Tora, and Fitz followed the compass needle to the shoreline.

When they reached the water, Isla looked out to the sea. There wasn't much to look at, except a giant rock that sat just beyond where the waves broke.

"Hmmm," Fitz hummed to himself. "I guess it makes sense that Fabio's teacher is a . . . rock."

"If his teacher's from the sea and the sailor's compass led us here," Isla said, "then I think you've got it from here, Tora."

Tora smiled at her friends. "There's only one way to call a mermaid, after all."

Holding the compass to her heart, Tora cleared her throat and sang.

Her beautiful voice soared from land to sea. It was as if Tora was calling the water to her. Isla noticed even passing hermit crabs stopped to stare in awe. Flying seagulls circled above them.

When she was done singing, Tora bowed.

They waited. And waited. And waited some more.

"Guys, look! The compass!" Tora said. In her hands, the compass suddenly started to shift. The needle moved away from the sea and now faced Tora!

"Huh . . ." Tora shook the old thing. "Maybe it *is* broken."

"I don't think so," Isla said. "I think this compass knows a mermaid's voice when it hears one. Nature is a mystery, just like Abuelo said!"

Tora beamed and hugged Isla. "I think today's real mystery was how well Fabio can sing."

Isla laughed. "The wildest mystery of them all!"

"Let's take a picture here. I never want to forget this day," Tora said. "Fitz, come stand between our shoulders."

"Coming, coming!" Fitz ended up squished between the girls.

"Okay," said Tora. "Everyone say *LAAAAAAAAAAAAA* on the count of three! One, two, three!"

"*LAAAAAAAAAAAAAA!*" they shouted.

When the photo printed out, Tora burst out laughing. "Fitz, were you falling asleep?"

Sure enough, Fitz's eyes were halfway closed.

His cheeks turned red. "Hey, I have been trying to steal a few gecko minutes to nap all day!"

But there was something else Isla noticed. "Guys, look!"

On the rock behind them, a long, graceful fin was diving back into the water.

Tora tilted the picture this way and that. "It could be a fish."

Isla threw her arm around her friend's shoulder. "Or it could be a mermaid. Who's to say? Nature is a mystery, after all."

Tora put her arm around Isla too. "I can see why you love this island so much. I think I'm going to love it for a long time."

That was the beauty of Sol. Every day, there was something new to discover.

DON'T MISS ISLA'S NEXT ADVENTURE!

HERE'S A SNEAK PEEK!

◆◆◆◆◆◆◆◆◆◆◆◆◆◆

Who loved to follow Isla Verde around the island of Sol, was very green, and would simply *not* stop talking?

Mia the iguana!

Isla and Fitz had been sitting on the curb of their neighborhood park when Mia stomped by, grumbling to herself. As soon as she'd spotted Isla, well . . . she'd stayed for a chat.

"The injustice!" Mia cried out. She paced back and forth angrily. "The nerve! The unfairness of it all! Oh, cruel world!"

Isla hid a laugh behind her coconut ice cream cone. If there was a contest to crown the most talkative reptile on the island, Mia would win every single time. But Isla kind of liked that about Mia. You could learn a lot from a reptile.

Fitz groaned as he lay on Isla's knee. Unlike Isla, he did *not* like the eternal chatter.

"It is way too hot outside to be this angry," Fitz said. "What's happening, and how does it affect me?"

Isla offered Fitz some of her frozen treat. "Something about another iguana stealing her favorite shady tree spot."

Mia huffed and puffed, her nails click-clacking with each step. "Why, don't you know how sensitive my scales are? It's not like I just wake up looking this beautiful in the morning. I need my shady tree canopy!"

Isla knew a large tree canopy was very important. It kept the ground cool for animals.

"Here's a wild idea," Fitz said. "Just find another tree."

"Fitz is right, Mia," Isla said. "Have you looked to see if a tree near you is up for grabs?"

"On the beach? All taken!" Mia sighed.

That made sense. The beach was a total hot spot.

Suddenly, Fitz straightened up. "Hey, what about the rain forest? My cousin is always moving around in there."

Mia gasped in delight. "Fitz, you are brilliant! Simply brilliant, my dear!"

He winked at Isla. "Oh, I get it from my best friend."